# THE NEXT STEP

## THE ROAD TO REGIONALS
## BOOK SIX

Adapted By
CHLOE VAN KEEKEN

BEACHWOOD
CANYON
PRODUCTIONS

For information go to **www.beachwoodcanyonproductions.com**

Printed in Canada

First Edition - November 2014

Book Design:  Rebecca Lasagna
Cover Design:  Yim Hung Kung

ISBN-978-0-9938500-5-9

# CHAPTER 1

## Emily

For the first time in a long time, Emily felt like everything at *The Next Step* was back to normal. As they rehearsed their Regionals' routine, practising full-out, Emily felt like this was a team that could actually win.

Every movement was perfectly placed, and everyone's timing was spot-on. The boys were jumping higher than they ever had, and the girls were adding extra sassiness to their group choreography. The dance had so many different intricate moves and styles that even Emily was impressed.

She was ashamed at how long it had taken her to realize it, but there certainly were more talented dancers than her. In fact, she may be the least-talented one in A-Troupe. At least, that was how she felt, standing on the sidelines during the acrobatics section.

All of the other dancers could do some type of acro, but Emily had never done anything more than a cartwheel. She had never felt the need to flip herself upside down, and if she was being honest, she still didn't.

But that was the best thing about being at *The Next Step*. She was allowed to have weaknesses. As long as everyone tried their hardest to support the team, they were welcome.

As the team struck a final pose and held it for a beat, Emily tried to catch her breath. They had all danced their absolute best, and despite everything they had been through, they were right on track to win Regionals.

"Good job, everybody! I loved the energy in that one!" Emily said, giving the team a round of applause. She could tell everyone was feeling as confident about Regionals as she was.

"You know what? Let's go home early tonight!" Emily suggested to the dancers. "How does that sound?"

"So good!" West said, high-fiving James and Eldon at the same time.

"I can't believe you're letting everyone go home early." Stephanie said.

"Well, I wouldn't want to wear everyone out before Regionals, would I?" Emily told Stephanie, smiling.

"Someone's learning." Stephanie said with a smile.

Things between Emily and Stephanie hadn't gotten completely back to normal. Emily knew that leaving Stephanie behind, when she was accepted at *Elite*, had really damaged their friendship, but she hoped that they could get back to being best friends again.

"Where do you guys think you're going?" Kate asked, stopping the dancers as she came out of her office.

"Home." West said, as he picked up his dance bag from the floor.

"Yeah, everyone did such a good job today, and the energy was great in that last run-through. So I thought we could let them go home early." Emily said, stepping up to defend her decision to Kate.

"Oh, the energy was great, huh?" Kate asked, crossing her arms. "No. We're not done here."

"What?" Michelle asked, clearly on the same page as Emily.

Emily wasn't sure what was going on. Kate had never interfered like this before.

"Joking!" Kate called out. "But you guys aren't leaving quite yet. You've been working so hard that I thought it was about time you all hung out together, as friends, not as teammates."

"I don't think we've ever done that before." Emily offered to the other dancers.

"I'm in!" West called out.

"Me, too!" Giselle said.

It seemed like everyone liked the idea of spending some time together as friends.

"Why don't you guys all get changed and get comfortable, and then meet back here for the festivities!" Kate told everyone.

As Emily headed off to the change room, she couldn't wait to see what tonight would bring.

# CHAPTER 2
## West

West was the last one out of the change rooms. He checked himself out in the mirror as he did a quick spin. There was no doubt about it, he looked like a cool dude.

"Okay, everybody, let's have some fun!" West called, as he pushed the doors open and headed into Studio-A.

The other dancers began laughing. West looked around to see that everyone was wearing their normal clothes. Why wasn't anyone else in their pyjamas?

"West, are those your pyjamas?" Emily asked him.

"Well, if you must know, yes, these are my pyjamas." West said. "Kate told us to get comfortable."

### E-Girl Rule #64

An E-Girl never leaves her house wearing pyjamas.

"Not that comfortable." Emily said, laughing along with the other dancers.

"Oh please, I am working this." West told Emily, as he straightened out his brightly coloured robe.

The dancers all laughed, as West sashayed around the dance floor like a runway model.

"Are you guys ready to have some fun?" Kate asked the dancers. "Why don't we get started by playing the Machine Game?"

West loved the Machine Game. It was a game he used to play when he was younger, and he had never lost his fondness for it. One person started the Machine by doing sounds and movements that suited whatever the Machine was supposed to build. Then another person joined in, adding their own sounds and movements. This continued until everyone had joined in, and they had created a giant, crazy machine!

"I want you guys to make a Koala Pyjamas Pant Machine." Kate told them, shouting the first weird thing that came into her head.

West didn't want to be the first one on the floor. He knew the Machine Game well. If you went first, you had to do the same sound and gesture for a very long time. Once, when he was building a Screaming Machine, he completely lost his voice for a week after.

Instead, West watched as Michelle made her way into the middle of the dance floor, started doing a weird move, and making even weirder sounds. Emily was the next to join in. Everyone got a kick out of watching her making silly noises.

As each of his team members joined the Machine, West was reminded of how lucky he was to have such amazing teammates. Not only were they a good group of people, they were also endlessly talented.  At least they were when they weren't busy making Koala Pyjamas Pants!  West laughed at his friends and then joined the Machine, jumping up and down in the middle of the Machine yelling "Boo!"

"Amazing!" Kate called out, as the dancers finally broke out of their machine-movements and into fits of laughter.  "Now that you guys are all loosened up, go get something to eat, hang out, and enjoy your night!" Kate said.  "I'll be in the office finishing up some paperwork if you need me."  And with that, Miss Kate headed for her office.

"Snack time!" West called out, heading over to the snack table that Kate had set up.

The dancers followed him, and as everyone filled up on the pretzels and juice Kate had left out for them, Tiffany spoke up.  "Why don't we play Truth or Dare?"

"Okay!" West said, pretzels flying out of his mouth.

"All right, West, you can go first.  Truth or dare?" Tiffany asked him.

"Truth!" West replied.  "I have nothing to hide!"

"Ooh!  I have a good one!" Riley said.  "What's your biggest secret?"

West had to think about that for a second.  He didn't have many secrets, but there was that one thing he had never told anyone.  "I witnessed a bank robbery before." West told the other dancers calmly.

"What?" James said, as he laughed.

"Yeah.  I actually followed the robber and saw where he buried the money."

"You know where the money is?" James asked in awe.

"Yeah, but it was a couple of years ago, so who knows if it's still there... My turn!" West told the other dancers.

But no one was ready for West to continue. They were still trying to make sense of his truth. On one hand, it was a perfectly normal thing for West to say, because it was West. There was nothing ordinary about him. But, on the other hand, it was a really weird thing to say. Who had experiences like that? No one!

Everyone stood there silently. It was because they had no idea what to say or what to ask. But it didn't matter. Because, before anyone could ask a question, West had already moved on.

"Stephanie, truth or dare?" West asked her.

"Dare." Stephanie said with a smile.

# CHAPTER 3

## Stephanie

Stephanie always picked dare. It was much safer than truth. Stephanie knew she didn't need to bother the other A-Troupe dancers with her own drama. Her parents never being around was hardly as significant as Chloe not having enough money to dance, or Daniel hurting himself. Her parents left her enough money to pay for more than three trips to Regionals every time they went away. Nobody would care about the poor little rich girl.

"I double-dog dare you to go into *Squeezed* and order some drinks... using Tiffany as your arms." West said, rubbing his hands together like he had invented the best evil plan.

"What?" Stephanie asked West, unsure of what he was saying.

"We should all go and watch." Michelle chimed in.

"Yeah!" Giselle added.

"I still don't understand." Stephanie said, following everyone out of Studio-A and down the stairs to *Squeezed*.

Once they got there West explained how it would all work. "Here put your arms behind your back." Stephanie did it immediately. "Now, Tiffany, stand behind Stephanie, and put your arms through here." West said, guiding Tiffany's arms through the space between Stephanie's arms. Suddenly, Tiffany's arms had become Stephanie's arms.

"Be good!" Stephanie whispered to Tiffany as they walked towards the counter, the other A-Troupe dancers close behind them.

"Hello." Stephanie said to the woman at the counter, as Tiffany waved both of her hands. "I think I would like to have a strawberry– " But before Stephanie could finish placing her order, she saw lipstick in front of her. Tiffany must have gone into her purse and found it.

"Ahem." Stephanie said, clearing her throat loudly enough so that Tiffany could hear it. She didn't need Tiffany smearing brand new Brilliant Beet lipstick all over her face. It was supposed to be a twenty-four hour lip stain, and Stephanie wasn't sure whether or not it would come off!

But Tiffany either didn't hear her, or didn't care, because the lipstick was coming towards Stephanie's face. Stephanie tried to move her face away, but it didn't seem to matter.

"Right there, that's the spot!" West called out as Tiffany drew on Stephanie's cheek with the lipstick.

"A little higher up!" Eldon told Tiffany, as suddenly Stephanie's nose was covered in lipstick.

Stephanie couldn't help but laugh as Tiffany blindly tried to do her make-up. There was lipstick on Stephanie's nose, on her cheek, and even on her forehead. And the other dancers laughed, too, as Tiffany began making lipstick dots all over Stephanie's face. Even the lady at the counter was laughing along with them now.

Normally Stephanie would feel uncomfortable with everyone laughing at her, but she knew it was all in good fun. Stephanie never had siblings, she never had cousins, all she had was Emily and the E-Girls. When all of her friendships fell apart, Stephanie felt lost for a while, like she was once again without a real family.

But now, she felt like everyone in A-Troupe was her family. And even though every single one of her teammates was laughing at her right now, Stephanie knew that she wouldn't trade this moment for anything in the whole world.

# CHAPTER 4

# Riley

Riley was full of laughter as she and the other members of A-Troupe made their way back from *Squeezed* to Studio-A. They had never spent time like this, all together without the pressures of Regionals looming over their heads. And now that Emily was back, it finally felt like their team was whole again. Riley couldn't wait for things to get completely back to normal.

"Who wants to watch a movie?" Kate asked the dancers as they re-entered Studio-A.

"Yes!" Riley cheered.

"Okay, this is what I've got: action-adventure, horror, or romantic comedy." Kate said, looking through the DVDs in her hands.

"Rom-com!" Giselle yelled out, clapping her hands along with Chloe and Stephanie. Giselle loved romantic comedies.

Riley knew exactly what she wanted to watch, but she didn't want to say it out loud. Her favourite movie was an old movie from the eighties that her mom had made her watch as a kid. She loved it, but she wasn't sure if anyone else would.

"Why don't we have a little dance-off?" Kate suggested. "Whoever does the best move, gets to pick which movie we watch."

"I'm out." Emily said, sitting down on the bench.

"Me, too. I don't really care." Michelle said, joining Emily.

"Me either." Riley joined in, sitting down beside the other two girls. She did care, but she wasn't interested in having to win a dance contest to get to pick.

"Well, I want to go!" West said, taking the floor.

"Go West! Go West!" Michelle, Emily, and Riley cheered as West broke out into a funky Moon Walk, waving his arms to match the motion of his feet.

Riley could never have imagined this moment would happen. She and Emily were laughing together and getting along like they used to so long ago. And now Michelle was joining them like they had been friends from the start.

Riley clapped as Giselle took the floor and announced that she had two moves. Riley couldn't believe that Giselle had thought up two brand new dance moves during the short amount of time West had been dancing. And both of her moves were completely original, acrobatic moves.

Finally, James stepped up to floor. Riley couldn't wait to see what he would do. She knew if James won, they would be stuck watching some terrible action movie with, at least, three car chases and fifteen explosions. But James's move was the most original. He modified a simple hand spin, using one hand and a lot of attitude. It was clear to Riley and everyone else that James had won this one.

"So, James, what do you want to watch?" Kate asked, clapping along with the other dancers as James took a bow.

"Hmm… Well, definitely not a romantic comedy!" James joked, looking at Giselle. Giselle stuck her tongue out at James.

The last time James had taken Riley to the movies, he had forced her to watch something about a robot-cop in space. It was three hours long, and there wasn't a single human in it.

"But to be totally honest, I don't really care. Why don't you choose, Riley?" James said, looking over at her.

"Awwww." the rest of A-Troupe called out.

"That's so cute!" Eldon cried in his best girlie voice.

Riley smiled as her face went red. "What about *Touchdowns and Tutus*?" Riley suggested, quickly trying to cover. "It's all about the exquisite beauty of a bunch of football players finding their inner beauty through ballet."

"Yes!" Emily agreed, clapping her hands together.

"I love that movie!" West chimed in. "My favourite part is when the two football players have to drag a boat up the Amazon River."

"What about when one of the players runs so fast he goes through a time warp?" Michelle added.

"And when the guy gets turned into a dog! And all the football players have to come together to rescue him from the dog pound." Stephanie said, laughing along with everyone else. "The director of that movie is crazy!"

Riley was surprised when everyone else agreed. She didn't realize that everyone else loved the wacky movie as much as she did!

As they all sat down to watch the movie, Riley realized this was the most fun she had had in a very long time.

# CHAPTER 5

## Emily

"Best movie ever." Emily said, clapping as *Touchdowns and Tutus* ended.

"You're welcome. You're welcome." Riley said, standing up to take a bow. James quickly pulled her back down beside him, and everyone laughed.

Emily loved how well everyone was getting along.

"Okay, I think we should get back to Truth or Dare." Tiffany suggested. "Since only a few people went last time."

"And I'd love to see someone top my dare." Stephanie added.

"I'll do it." James offered. "I take dare."

"Okay!" Tiffany said, smiling.

Emily saw the gleam in Tiffany's eye. She had known Tiffany for long enough to know that she had something up her sleeve.

"I dare you to kiss Riley." Tiffany said, giggling.

"No! I do not want to see that." Emily cried, covering her eyes. She didn't need to see her little sister kiss anyone.

"Oh come on, that's too easy." James said, turning his head and giving Riley a quick peck on the lips.

Even though Emily thought James and Riley's relationship was adorable, she was glad things weren't like that between her and Eldon. They were much more private about their feelings.

"Okay, Emily, truth or dare?" James asked her.

"Dare." Emily said confidently. She knew she was

always better off with a dare than a truth.

"I dare you to do the *Six Cracker Challenge*." James told Emily.

"What is that?" Emily asked, confused.

"You have to try to eat six crackers in one minute, without any water." James answered.

"No. I'm not doing that." Emily insisted, now that she knew what they were talking about. Eldon had shown her videos of people doing the same thing online, and as it turns out, no one was actually able to do it.

"You have to do what you're dared. I still have lipstick on my face." Stephanie reminded her.

Emily knew Stephanie was right. Stephanie had embarrassed herself as a part of the game, and if Emily had to do something similar, so be it. That was what tonight was about, having fun with her friends.

"Here, I had some crackers in my bag." West said, pulling a half empty sleeve of crackers out of his dance bag. He counted out six and placed them in Emily's hands.

"Do it! Do it! Do it!" the girls chanted, in an effort to encourage Emily.

"On your mark, get set, salt!" James called out, and Emily started shoving crackers into her mouth. There was no way she would be able to do this dare gracefully, so she

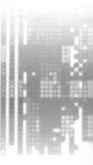

might as well make herself look as silly as possible to make everyone else laugh.

Emily shoved the last cracker in her mouth and raised her arms over her head triumphantly.

"Okay, now say the alphabet!" Riley called out.

"A, B, C, D..." Emily began, as pieces of cracker flew out of her mouth and all over Stephanie.

"Ew! It went in my hair!" Stephanie cried, as Emily tried not to laugh. But it was too late. Tears streamed down Emily's cheeks, as Stephanie jumped out of her seat, trying her hardest to get all of the pieces of cracker off of her.

"Here." Eldon said, handing Emily a bottle of water. She was so grateful she had her loyal boyfriend by her side, in the best of times, and the worst of times.

# CHAPTER 6
## Michelle

Michelle couldn't breathe, she was laughing so hard. She had never before seen Emily act that silly. It was the best part of her night so far. Once the laughter died down, Michelle wondered who would go next. She was having such a fun time hanging out with everyone that she didn't really care.

"Michelle, you haven't gone yet." Emily said, eyeing her from across the room.

Michelle scrunched up her nose. She really didn't want to do a dare, after what Emily and Stephanie had just done. So she knew her only other option was to tell the 'truth'.

"I'll take truth." she said.

"Out of all the guys in A-Troupe, who would you want to date the most?" Emily asked.

Michelle froze. She wondered for a moment if Emily somehow knew about her crush on Eldon? But when Michelle looked at Emily, she knew that things had changed too much. Emily may have been that sneaky before, but Emily was just playing the game like everyone else was, right? But how could Michelle possibly tell the truth? The entire party would go from fun to done in six seconds flat.

As she looked around at the group, trying to figure out who she should name, her eyes caught Eldon's. And for a brief second, she wished she could tell everyone the truth; that she liked Eldon and Eldon liked her, too.

But Michelle knew that could never happen. Not now that Emily had come back, and everything was going so well with the team.

"Um… West?" Michelle said to the room.

"That's right!" West said, standing up and squishing himself in between Michelle and Chloe. Michelle laughed. If she couldn't tell her team the truth, she was happy playing along with West's jokes. And with everyone laughing, no one suspected her true feelings.

# CHAPTER 7

# Eldon

Eldon saw the way Michelle had looked at him when Emily asked who Michelle might like. And with her look to him, he knew that she felt the same way he did. But what could either of them do about it?

Eldon was not sure, and it wasn't making things any easier being apart from Michelle. He knew he shouldn't try to talk to her about his feelings here at *The Next Step*, but he could not stop himself.

While the group took a quick water break, Eldon found Michelle standing alone. She had been avoiding him ever since Emily had gotten back from *Elite*. But Eldon was not going to let her off that easily, especially after she had looked at him in that way.

"What do you want?" Michelle asked him, as he approached her.

"I saw the look you gave me during Truth or Dare." Eldon told her.

"So what. Eldon, you're dating Emily. She's your girlfriend!" Michelle shot.

Eldon knew Michelle was right. If he was with Emily, he should not be pushing things with Michelle. But he did not care. He wanted to be with Michelle, not Emily. And he knew what he had to do.

"I'm going to break up with her." Eldon said, looking into Michelle's eyes, hoping she saw how serious he was.

But Michelle only frowned. "You can't do that." Michelle told him.

Eldon's heart sank. He had just told Michelle that he chose her over Emily. So why wasn't Michelle happy about it?

"Why not?" Eldon asked.

"One, you will break her heart." Michelle reminded him. "And two, if you break up with her, you will mess everything up for the team." For a second Eldon stared at Michelle. Her passion for doing what was best for the team was one of the things he liked about her, but right now it was driving him crazy.

"Who's hungry?" Eldon heard Emily call from across the floor.

Without giving him a second glance, Michelle walked away from Eldon and their potential relationship, and towards Emily and the team. He knew all of the reasons that he could not go chasing after her, but that did not stop him from wanting to do exactly that.

# CHAPTER 8

# Riley

"I'm starving!" Riley said, joining the rest of the team in the centre of the floor. It was true; they had been there for hours, and now it was time to eat.

"How about pizza?" Emily asked.

"Yes!" Riley said, agreeing along with the rest of A-Troupe. What was a party without pizza?

"I was thinking that we should tell some ghost stories." West said, shining a flashlight into his face and trying to make himself look scary.

"But everyone's hungry." Emily said, shooting a look to Riley. Emily knew how much Riley hated to be scared.

"How about whoever gets the most scared, buys the pizza? Boys against girls." James suggested.

"It's on!" Emily agreed.

Riley knew that once it became a challenge, there was no way Emily was going to turn it down. Riley just had to hope she could keep it together long enough to win a free pizza.

As everyone took their places in a circle, Stephanie started her story for the girls' side. "One night, a couple was driving down an old dirt road when they heard a story on the radio about a patient who had escaped from the local asylum." Stephanie began. "When their car broke down, the boyfriend went for help. A little while later, the girl heard a scratching on top of their car, but decided to wait until the boyfriend came back to see what it was. But after he hadn't come back for an hour, the girl got out of the car and–"

"The boyfriend's hanging from a tree and his feet are scraping across the roof." West interrupted.

"West!" Emily said, annoyed at the interruption.

"Oh, come on, we've all heard that one." West told Emily.

It was true, even Riley wasn't scared by that old ghost story.

"All right, West, you got this?" James said, as he got out of his seat.

"Where are you going?" Riley asked James.

"To get some more snacks."

"We just ordered pizza!" Riley said, rolling her eyes.

"I'm a growing boy!" James said, with a wink to the other boys, as he casually sauntered out of Studio-A.

Riley liked James a great deal, but sometimes he could get on her nerves. Did he really need snacks right at this very minute?

"What are you guys up to?" Kate asked, as she entered the studio.

"Telling ghost stories. I was just about to tell mine." West told Kate.

"All right, I want to listen to this!" Kate said excitedly, taking James's old seat.

"Now, before I tell you this story, I wanted to let you know that this building used to be a chicken processing factory." West began.

Riley immediately tensed up. She hated chickens.

"He's lying." Emily said to everyone, but Riley couldn't help but think her sister was trying to make Riley feel better.

"It's true!" West exclaimed.

"He's right." Kate cut in. "Haven't you guys ever noticed the chickens on the wall?" Kate said, gesturing to the back of the studio.

Everyone turned to look at the faded chickens painted on the wall.

"I honestly just thought that was for decoration." Michelle said.

Riley had never thought much about the old chickens painting. In fact, she specifically tried to never look at it.

When Riley was younger, her parents took her to a petting zoo for her birthday. She had begged all day to feed the chickens, and eventually her parents agreed, even though she was so small. But when she got in the chicken cage with the food in her hands, the chickens flocked around her and started pecking. Riley had screamed, until her dad came and picked her up, and scared all the chickens away.

West continued, making his voice sound low and serious, "So, back in 1922, there were a lot of chickens in this building. And before they would be taken in to be processed, they lived in this very room." West continued.

"Well, I hope we got new floors." Emily said, trying to make light of the situation.

But it was too late. Riley shivered as she looked around at the room and imagined it full of chickens.

"The night before all the chickens were supposed to

be killed, one of the chickens managed to pick the lock on the cage using its beak. And then it got out and undid all the other locks on all the other cages."

"No way!" said Riley.

"Yup, it was a really smart chicken." nodded West. And so all of the chickens escaped. It took days for the people who owned the factory to catch all the chickens. They searched and searched until they got all of the chickens back. All except for one." West said, shining the flashlight in his face for a scary effect.

Riley felt a chill go through her body.

"Was it was the chicken who knew how to pick the lock?" asked Riley. She was completely panicked by now.

"Yes. And one night, while the security guard was sleeping, the one missing chicken… PECKED THE GUARD TO DEATH!" West ended with a flourish.

"Oh, my." said Riley.

"No." Emily said immediately.

"That's not even realistic." Stephanie cut in.

It didn't matter whether the story was real or not. Riley was starting to feel like she could see chickens everywhere.

"But it's true. And they never caught that last chicken. And, to this day, if you listen closely--"

"Rawr!" Riley heard behind her.

As she turned around she saw it: THE EVIL CHICKEN! It was here! And it was right behind her! And it was about to attack her. Riley screamed, jumped out of her seat, and ran halfway across the room. By the time she had turned around, everyone was laughing.

"That wasn't funny!" Riley shouted at James, who had by now, removed the head of a bird costume he was wearing.

"Oh, come on, this isn't even a chicken costume. It's a

pigeon!" James said good-naturedly.

"Guess who's paying for the pizza?!" laughed West.

Riley had had enough for one night. James knew she was terrified of chickens. The boys must have had this planned the whole time. She ran out of Studio-A to get some air. It was the only way she wouldn't lose it on James. He had been pushing her more and more, and it was starting to get on Riley's nerves.

"You guys really know how to take things too far." Riley heard Emily yell at the boys, before turning around to follow her.

Riley stopped just outside the doors of Studio-A to wait for Emily. As soon as she saw her sister come around the corner Riley said, "We have to get them back."

"Don't you worry, I already have a plan." Emily said, as she smiled and put her arm around her sister.

Riley smiled as she walked down the hall with Emily. It was the first time things were back to normal between the two sisters, and Riley was grateful.

# CHAPTER 9

## Emily

Emily smiled as she paid the pizza man. The boys might have gotten Riley, but the girls had a plan that would freak out all of the boys, especially James.

As Giselle distracted the boys, the other girls blocked the pizza from view and doused the entire thing with hot sauce. Sure, it wasn't the most original prank, but Emily knew it would distract the boys so that they wouldn't suspect their real prank.

"Pizza's here!" Emily called, as they brought the pizza into Studio-A.

"Pizza!" West called. He and the other boys flocked around the pizza boxes Emily carried in.

"Wait up." James said, opening the first box of pizza. "That has hot sauce on it."

"No, it doesn't." Emily said, trying to cover.

"My mom puts hot sauce on everything. I can smell hot sauce from a mile away. Which meant I could smell it while you were putting it on the pizza." James told the girls.

"Not only did you guys try to play a prank on us," West said, picking up a slice of pizza and taking a giant bite, "you actually made this pizza better!" West shoved the rest of the slice in his mouth.

"We just knew you liked hot sauce." Emily said, trying to pretend that their plan had been ruined.

As the boys began eating, the girls all looked at each other. All they had to do now was wait. But they didn't have to wait for long.

The studio doors swung open. "What are you guys doing here? No one is supposed to be here this late." an imposing male police officer entered, sternly asking the dancers.

"No, no, we're here with our teacher." James said, stepping in like the confident man he thought he was. This was exactly what the girls had been hoping would happen.

"Kate?" Emily called out, but Kate was nowhere to be found. She had disappeared at Emily's request.

"I don't see any teacher." the police officer told the dancers.

"Honestly, there is nothing here to worry about." James said to the police officer.

"Don't tell me what to worry about!" the police officer yelled at James. James tried to smile back. "And wipe that smile off your face." The police officer glared at James.

Emily could barely contain her laughter. As she looked around at the other girls, she could tell she wasn't the only one. All of the boys looked terrified.

"Are you trying to impress your friends? How impressive do you think it's going to be when Mommy and Daddy have to come down to the station to pick you up?" the police officer asked James.

Emily had never seen James so nervous before. For someone who was usually so cool and composed, he certainly didn't have it all under control now.

"Okay, I don't think that's necessary." West said, stepping in to help his friend.

"Was I talking to you?" the police officer shot back.

Without a word, West stepped back to where he was standing.

"Turn around, hands behind your back." the police officer ordered James, who was now too scared not to obey. As James turned around, the police officer smacked him on the head and the girls began laughing.

"I can't do it anymore!" the police officer said, laughing.

"Uncle Mel, I think we got them!" Giselle said, stepping forward.

"We got you!" Emily said, laughing along with all of the other girls.

"Okay, I admit it. The double prank was genius!" James said, joining in on the laughter. He was so relieved.

"What's going on in here?" Kate asked with a smile, returning to Studio-A.

"Wait, Miss Kate, were you in on this?" James asked, stunned.

But Miss Kate only shrugged. Emily knew she would never give the girls away. Sometimes the boys needed to learn a lesson, even if it was a little one.

"So, what do you guys say to ending the night with a dance party?" Kate asked, turning on the music.

Emily watched as the rest of her team began to bust a move on the dance floor. Spending the night together like this really proved to Emily how much more than teammates they all were. They were also friends.

Emily looked around at each and every dancer in the studio. She realized that she had known all of them a long time. She had spent more time with some of the dancers than she had with her own family. They actually were her family, many of them dancing with her since they were three years old . Then Emily looked over at Riley. She was truly happy for her sister. Riley had really grown up during these past several months. She even had a boyfriend now. And speaking of boyfriends, Emily looked over at Eldon. He was dancing next to Michelle. Emily felt like the luckiest girl in the world. With Eldon at her side, she was ready for anything. And more than that, they were all ready for Regionals.

# CHAPTER 10

# Daniel

Daniel stood outside the door to Studio-A. It had been far too long since he had opened that door. Usually he was in a hurry to get to rehearsal, and he never gave the door much thought. But it seemed different today. It seemed heavier: a barrier to a world in which he no longer had a role.

He hated the fact that he had injured himself. He played the lift over and over in his head. Had he not set his feet properly? Was he using his arms to lift, instead of his legs? Should he have warmed up more? He had done the lift so many times, it was hard to know exactly what had gone wrong.

But now Daniel just stood outside the door, unable to open it. He had decided to come wish *The Next Step* dancers good luck on their trip to Regionals. He knew it would be hard to see everyone. And he certainly didn't want everyone fawning over him because he was hurt. He was so not into drama. But Daniel did want to show everyone he was a team player. So he steeled himself, and finally went through the door, unsure of how he would feel when he saw the dancers packed up and ready to get on the bus. But when Daniel walked through the door, the A-Troupers were not there. It was only J-Troupe, and they seemed like they were about to perform a song. Noah stood behind a microphone with a guitar slung around him, Camille held a tambourine, Chad was on drums, and Lily stood at a keyboard. What was going on? Had *The Next*

30

*Step* turned into a music studio?

Just then, Gabi from J-Troupe, burst through the doors and shouted, "They're coming!"

As the J-Troupers readied themselves to perform, all the A-Troupers entered. And when they saw Daniel, they all rushed to hug him, genuinely concerned with how he was doing. Daniel couldn't help but grin. He was so happy for them. And more importantly, relieved that he felt happy.

As J-Troupe sang a goodbye song for A-Troupe, and everyone danced around the studio, Daniel realized how lucky he was to be a part of *The Next Step*. He wished them well at Regionals, and he really hoped that they would win. Because if they did, Daniel swore that he was going to get a spot on A-Troupe for Nationals. He would work hard, get his solo back, and everything would get back on track. Go *Next Step*!

# CHAPTER 11

## Michelle

Michelle felt a shiver go up her spine as she stepped onto the Regionals' stage. It wasn't her first time here, but it was the first time with *The Next Step*. A-Troupe had gone through so much this year. It was amazing they had made it to Regionals in one piece.

"Giselle is here!" Giselle called out to the empty auditorium, as she dropped her bags and headed into the middle of the stage.

"Michelle is here, too!" Michelle said, mimicking Giselle.

"And so is West!" West chimed in.

Michelle laughed as she watched the rest of her team explore the stage. She couldn't believe how hard they had all worked, so that they could be here right now: Chloe had to waitress at a restaurant in order to pay her way. James had to work on his math so that he could stay in A-Troupe. Daniel had rehearsed so hard he had hurt himself, and his chances of a future career in dance. And Emily and Michelle had started off as enemies, but eventually came together to become good friends and great Co-Captains.

And then there was Eldon… He stood beside Michelle on stage. She could feel his arm graze hers. She instinctively reached out for his hand, and then remembered that he wasn't her boyfriend. He was Emily's. So she stopped herself.

Michelle looked up, and Eldon, who was looking back at her, smiled. A warm feeling filled Michelle's body. She liked him so much. Why did he have to be Emily's boyfriend? Couldn't Michelle find someone else to like?

But she knew the truth. She liked Eldon, and Eldon liked her. How was she supposed to keep pretending any differently? Because that's what was best for the team. The team Michelle had fought to be on, from the moment she had set foot in *The Next Step Studio*. And everything was working like it should. Michelle and Emily were finally allies instead of enemies, and the rest of the team was really responding to their joint leadership.

So why was it, now that everything was calm, Michelle's crush on Eldon had to rear its head? It had taken Emily ages to forgive Michelle for 'stealing' her Dance Captaincy. It would take a lot longer, maybe forever, for Emily to forgive her for 'stealing' her boyfriend. The only thing Michelle could do was ignore Eldon. Maybe after enough time, their feelings for each other would go away.

# CHAPTER 12

## Emily

Emily tried to shake off the image of Eldon and Michelle smiling at each other. Eldon and Michelle were dance partners, and friends, and that was it. Or that was what Emily chose to believe.

As *The Next Step* dancers waited in the foyer of the theatre to register, Emily busied herself with thoughts of the competition: Would all of their costumes fit properly? Did the sound technician have their music? Was there anything Emily had forgotten?

Emily was so distracted by her thoughts that she only noticed Amanda, the Dance Captain of *Elite*, as she brushed past Emily. When Emily looked up, all of the *Elite* dancers, dressed in matching tracksuits, rudely marched through *The Next Step* dancers, and right to the front of the registration line.

"Why do they get to cut the line?" West asked.

Emily knew everyone was thinking the same thing as West. "Because *Elite* won last year, so they get priority registration." Emily explained. It was a dumb rule. Unless *The Next Step* won. Then it would seem like a good rule.

Emily braced herself as Amanda returned. Emily hadn't seen or spoken to Amanda since she had left *Elite*. She hadn't exactly left them on the best of terms. Or any terms at all. After she had overheard them talking about kicking her off the team, Emily had gone straight home and made her dad switch her back to *The Next Step*.

"Are you enjoying waiting in line?" Amanda asked

snidely.

"Actually, I am. I'm with my team." Emily said, facing Amanda dead-on. She wasn't scared of her anymore.

"Oh, please," Amanda scoffed, "I bet you wish you were still at *Elite*."

"You know what? I think I'm okay here." Emily said, looking Amanda right in the eyes. She knew that Amanda was just trying to intimidate her. It was standard operating procedure at *Elite*. And the only reason it didn't affect Emily was because she used to be an E-Girl. And, she had to admit to herself, being an E-Girl had certainly toughened her up for things like this.

"Actually, Emily is fine here. And we don't need matching jackets to prove we're a team." Michelle said, stepping up to stand beside Emily.

Emily appreciated the support. Standing up to Amanda wasn't easy, and Emily was willing to take any help that she could get. Emily thought the matching tracksuit line Michelle said to Amanda was perfect.

"We do have matching socks though." West said, stepping up to stand on Emily's other side.

"West!" Emily heard her entire team groan. This was not the time or place for West's jokes.

"You guys are a joke." Amanda sneered, as she flipped her hair and headed off to be with her team.

"Boy, Amanda really is intense." Riley said, watching Amanda rejoin her team.

"It doesn't matter." Emily said, rolling her eyes and turning back towards her team. "We have to take *Elite* down." Everyone there agreed.

# CHAPTER 13

# West

West stood in the foyer with the rest of *The Next Step*, looking at the bracket board. It showed the twenty-four teams competing at Regionals. As Kate explained the rules of Regionals, she pointed to different parts of the board.

"Everyone pay attention so we know what we're up against. There are twenty-four teams in this competition." Kate explained. "Three brackets of eight teams."

For West this was easy to understand. "Do you get that, James?" he said. "Three brackets, with eight teams in each bracket. Three times eight, equals twenty-four."

James laughed. Yes, even he could understand the rules so far.

"In each bracket of eight teams, Regionals starts with four teams competing against the other four teams in the bracket." Miss Kate continued.

"Does that mean that after the first round, only the four winning teams in each bracket continue on?" West asked.

"Yes, exactly." Kate said. "In our bracket the four winning teams then compete against each other--"

"Leaving two teams in each bracket." West said. He saw James looking at him with a slightly confused look on his face, and thought how amazed James must be at his mathematical prowess. West continued, "And then those two teams compete, leaving a winner of that bracket!" West had a look on his face that seemed to say it was all easy-peasy-lemon-squeezy. "Let me guess, Miss Kate,"

West continued smugly, "the winner of each of the three brackets move on to the semi-finals and compete against each other?"

Then Kate surprised even West. "Yes, but that's only three teams moving forward. Don't you need a fourth team to have semi-finals?"

Everyone scratched their heads. Kate was right. You did need four teams to have a semi-finals. And not even West knew the answer to Kate's question.

But then James surprised everyone. "That's where the wildcard spot comes in." Everyone looked at James, especially Riley. She was impressed.

"That's right, James." Kate said. "Would you care to explain?"

"I'll try." James said, almost nervously. "In every round that a team competes in, they get points from the judges. And, after the three bracket winners are determined, the next three teams that have gotten the most points are eligible to get the wildcard spot and move on to the final spot in semi-finals."

Everyone looked at Kate to see what she would say. "You are correct, sir." Kate said.

Everyone was really impressed with James.

"And what decides what team makes it?" Emily asked.

"It's up to the judges. It's a combo of points, how good the dances were, their attitude. You know, you gotta bring it." James said. Everyone laughed.

Kate continued, "And that means that the more rounds our team wins, and the more points we get each round, then the better it is for us if we need to win the wildcard slot."

"Like if we lose in the first round, there's no way we're getting the wildcard spot, right James?" West pressed.

"I don't know." James laughed.

"Then how did you know about the wildcard spot?" Riley asked.

"I looked it up online during the bus ride here. What? We had a lot of time to kill." Everyone laughed. That's how James knew what was going on.

West was about to laugh, too. But then, out of the corner of his eye, he noticed his friend Marcel. What was Marcel doing at Regionals? *Seeds* had never competed in an official competition before. They were a street crew, not a competitive dance team.

West moved closer to where Marcel and the rest of *Seeds* had gathered. He watched as the local reporter, who had come out to cover Regionals, asked Marcel for an interview. West took a few steps closer so he could hear what they said.

"I'm here with Marcel, captain of *Seeds*, a well-known street dance crew. Now, word on the street is you only have nine dancers registered right now. Is that true?" the reporter asked.

"That is true. Our tenth dancer, Tony, is running a little late, but he will be here soon." Marcel answered, trying to sound confident.

But West knew his old friend too well. Marcel was nervous.

"Now what the viewers at home don't know is, all teams here at the *Absolute Dance Regionals* must have ten dancers registered in order to compete." the reporter continued. "So if Tony doesn't show up, your team will be disqualified."

"He'll show up." Marcel said, staring straight into the camera. The interview ended, and Marcel headed off backstage. His team would be performing soon.

West didn't want to see his old team have to forfeit. He

could only imagine how hard they all had to work in order to get themselves to the competition. *Seeds* not being able to perform would be an injustice, not only to *Seeds,* but to the whole dance world.

West returned to his team, wondering the best way to ask them for their permission to do what he had to do. "I really need to talk to you guys about something." West told his teammates, "*Seeds* is missing a member of their troupe."

"Well, that's perfect. One less team to beat." Riley pointed out.

But West didn't feel the same way.

"I kind of want to fill their empty spot and dance for them." West said, hoping the rest of the team would understand.

"Are you crazy?" Emily asked him. "No, absolutely not, you came here with us, you're dancing with us." Emily asserted.

"But *Seeds* is in a completely different bracket." West told his teammates. "We wouldn't even be competing against them until semi-finals, and, by that time, Tony will be back."

"Why do you want to dance with them anyway?" Giselle asked him.

"Because I used to dance with them. Before I came to *The Next Step,*" West told them honestly, "they were my family. I just feel like I owe it to them. You know, for leaving."

"*Elite* would never let one of their own dancers compete with another studio." Riley reminded them.

"You guys, obviously we're not *Elite.*" Michelle reminded everyone.

West looked around at the other dancers, hoping someone would see his side.

"You know what," Emily said, breaking the silence, "Michelle's right, we're not *Elite*. Michelle, how do you feel about a vote?" Emily asked.

"I think a vote is a good idea." Michelle confirmed.

"Okay, those for West dancing for *Seeds*, for this round only, raise your hand." Emily asked the dancers.

West smiled as almost everyone raised their hands. But he was surprised it was Emily who was the first one to really support him.

"Looks like you are good to go, West." Emily said.

"But we are on at three, and if you are not back here in time, I swear..." Emily said, back to her super-serious self.

"Don't worry! I'll be back. I promise." West said, as he ran off to find Marcel and the rest of *Seeds*. He couldn't wait to tell them the good news.

**Marcel** — 4.22PM

Here I come to save the day!

We don't need your help, Compass.

Then help me out, because I'd really like to be there for my friends.

...

Backstage, NOW!

# CHAPTER 14

## Michelle

Michelle snuck into the back of the theatre with the rest of *The Next Step* dancers to watch West perform with *Seeds*. They all knew how good *Seeds* were. West had shown them videos of different dance battles *Seeds* had posted online.

As good as West was, Michelle still felt a little uneasy about watching him dance with another troupe. There was always the chance he could get injured while he was dancing. And then what would they do? As the lights came up and the music began, West immediately backflipped his way into the spotlight. *Seeds* was good, but West was clearly the best dancer on stage. Michelle was glad that, after all was said and done, West would be on her team.

"Okay, guys, let's go get dressed." Kate said, ushering *The Next Step* dancers out of the auditorium.

It was minutes later, and the team was entering their dressing rooms. "And *Seeds* wins the round with eighty-eight points." Michelle overheard. There was a small TV set in the corner of the room that showed what was happening on stage. Michelle and the other girls watched, as West celebrated his victory with the *Seeds* dancers. Nobody said anything, but Michelle could guess what everyone was thinking: *Seeds* had just made it one step closer to becoming Regionals' champions.

Suddenly, everyone remembered what they were supposed to be doing. Michelle picked up her hairbrush, and the girls rushed around, putting on their costumes and helping each other with their make-up. There was an excitement about competition time that motivated Michelle. With everyone rushing with their own preparations, Michelle could feel the electricity in the air.

Competition was where the dancers got to show what they could do, not only to each other, but also to prospective dance schools and scholarship programs. A good performance at competition meant a total leg-up in the dance world.

As a finishing touch, the girls all lined up in front of Stephanie, and she painted the perfect winged eyeliner and plump red pout on each of them. Michelle was glad they had a near-professional make-up artist on their team.

"Yo! Let's go!" Michelle heard James call, as he knocked and opened the door to their dressing room.

"Where's West?" Michelle asked, as the girls followed James and Eldon up to the stage.

"He's not here yet." Eldon said, walking a little faster to catch up with her. "Maybe he's switching into our costume?"

Michelle walked ahead and joined the girls for a final look in the mirror. She was too worried about West to even think about Eldon right now. She just wished her cheeks felt the same way.

"Okay, gather around." Kate called out, as everyone formed a huddle around her.

"This is our first step on the road to Nationals." Kate told them.

Michelle smiled. She couldn't wait to go to Nationals with *The Next Step*. The studio had only been there once before, and that was a long time ago when Kate was in A-Troupe.

"Wait, where is West?" Emily asked.

"He's right there!" James pointed out.

Michelle looked to where James was pointing and saw West. For a second she was relieved, until she saw that he was LIMPING.

"Guys, I hurt my ankle when I was on stage with *Seeds*. I don't know if I'll be able to dance." West trailed off, in obvious pain.

Michelle's heart began to race. Was he serious? This was the exact thing they had all been worried about.

Stephanie shook her head. "This is the most ironic, worst thing that could ever happen to us. I don't even know what to say."

Giselle agreed, "How could this be happening to us?"

"Then why are you dressed, bro?" James asked.

"It's true." Michelle thought. West was dressed to perform. If he had injured himself, would he have done that?

West stared at them for a few seconds. "Okay! I'm kidding!" West said with a wide smile.

"I am going to kill you!" Emily said, giving West a

friendly punch. "I can't believe you would do that!"

"Come on, guys, I always land on my feet!" West

joked. "That's why the *Seeds* dancers call me Compass! Because I know all the directions."

"Okay, Compass, get in here! Everybody, hands in!" Kate told them. "*The Next Step* on three. One, two, three—"

"*The Next Step!*" Michelle yelled, throwing her hands in the air with the other A-Troupe dancers.

As they took the stage, Michelle held her head high. They had been waiting for this moment for so long, and it was finally here. This is what every drop of blood, sweat, and tears had been about.

This was Regionals.

# CHAPTER 15
# Riley

So far, *The Next Step* had won their first two rounds. They had been blowing away the competition, and Riley was feeling like they actually had a chance to win. All they had to do was win one more round, and they would be in the semi-finals.

Riley waited in the wings, watching *Dance, Inc.* perform. They were amazing, and their dance moves were completely in synch. When they scored eighty-five points, Riley knew that *The Next Step* had to perform perfectly, if they wanted to get a score high enough to move to the next round.

As Riley found her place on stage, she looked over at James. He smiled back at her. She didn't know how she would have made it through the past few months without him. He wasn't just her boyfriend. He was her best friend, too.

Their music started, and they sprung into motion. They had already performed their routine twice today, so by this point, they had the moves down perfectly.

As the girls sashayed across the stage one way, the boys double-toured across the stage the other way. The audience cheered, injecting the dancers with energy.

Riley pushed herself to dance harder with every clap she heard. As she danced the partner section with James, she felt like she was on top of the world. There was no way this moment could get any more perfect.

Riley smiled widely as she found her spacing for the

lyrical section. As she threw her arms around in front of her head, she felt a tug in her hair. She tried to move her right arm, but the lace glove she was wearing was caught in her hairpiece. Riley tried desperately to free herself, but as she tugged her hand free, the feather in her hair came flying out and landed on the stage.

For a moment, everything went white. It was as if time had stopped. It was like she was watching the whole thing from outside her body. She could no longer even hear the music. Finally, there was a loud rushing in her ears, a lump formed in her throat, and then reality crashed down on Riley. She quickly caught up with the routine, joining in a few beats later, trying to act as if nothing had happened. But Riley knew the damage had already been done. That small mistake she just made could cost them the entire competition. Losing a part of your costume, unless it was part of the routine, was a fault. And, at this stage of the competition, a fault meant your dreams were dashed. You would be going home.

All she wanted to do was to run off stage and hide, but she knew the only choice she had was to finish the routine. After what had just happened, she owed her team that much.

As they struck their final pose, James reached for her hand and continued to hold it while they waited to receive their score from the judges. But all Riley felt was numb. If they didn't score higher than eighty-five points, *The Next Step* would be out of the competition, and it would all be because of her.

"In their third round, *The Next Step* scores…" the announcer called out, as Riley held her breath.

"Eight-four points. *Dance, Inc.* moves on to the semi-finals, and *The Next Step* is eliminated." The words rang out loudly in the theatre, and the audience began a polite round of applause.

They had lost. Everything A-Troupe had endured to get to this moment had been for nothing. And Riley was to blame.

She couldn't take the bright lights or the sound of the audience. She bolted off stage, collapsing in a chair, unable to stand on her own weight any longer. But her team was close behind her, circling around her.

"My hand got caught… And then it fell out…" Riley said, trying to catch her breath through the tears. "And then we lost because of me, we just lost!" She couldn't stop herself from yelling. There was so much emotion inside of her, she felt like she might burst.

"Riley," Emily said, kneeling down in front of Riley and taking her hands, "it's fine. These things happen."

"But we were so close." Riley cried. She knew Emily was just being nice. She had to be just as disappointed as Riley, if not more. Everyone had to be.

"Everyone gave it their all. It happened, and there is nothing we can do about it now." Kate told her.

"I don't know why everyone is so upset." James said.

Riley couldn't believe what James was saying. How could he not see why they were all disappointed? "James, really?" Riley snapped. She so wasn't in the mood for James's nonchalant attitude.

But James just smiled. "The last time I checked, we still had a chance at the wildcard spot. And we're obviously going to get it, so everyone can calm down, just a little bit."

"You know what? For once, James is right." Emily said, standing up.

Riley wasn't sure if she had just heard her sister correctly. Had Emily just said that James was right about something?

"We worked too hard not to make it to Nationals." Emily said.

"I'm sorry, guys." Riley said, without thinking. She couldn't help herself; she felt horrible.

"STOP!" the other A-Troupe dancers smiled back at her. She had a feeling they weren't going to let her feel horrible for long.

# CHAPTER 16

## Emily

It didn't matter that Emily was disappointed. She had to remain positive for the sake of the team. It was her job as Dance Co-Captain to keep her eye on the prize.

So Emily didn't give Amanda, or the *Elite* dancers, a second look as they filed past *The Next Step*. *Elite* was on their way to the stage to start their semi-final dance. A-Troupe had decided to watch the teams performing that were vying for semi-final spots. *Dance, Inc.* had already made it in by beating *The Next Step*. There were still two spots to fill.

From the wings, Emily watched *Elite* dance. She knew the routine they were performing. It was the same one they were rehearsing when Emily was at *Elite*. Emily had been impressed with the dance even when it was performed in *Elite's* studio. But on the Regionals' stage, with the lighting and the costumes, Emily knew that *Elite's* routine would be better than ever.

As the *Elite* dance continued, Emily listened to her teammates gasp and groan. She knew they were all blown away by *Elite's* choreography.

"Did Amanda just break that guy's neck?" West asked Emily.

"Yeah, she's supposed to be a daemon or something." Emily said, rolling her eyes.

But it was obvious to everyone that not only was *Elite's* entire routine flawless, the concept of the dance was incredible as well. Amanda was a daemon that married a man, then discarded him. It was exactly what Amanda had done to Emily; invited her into *Elite*, with plans to toss her out unceremoniously. Emily was glad she had left before that had happened.

And when *Elite's* dance ended, it was no surprise to Emily that *Elite* got a score of ninety-four points. It was the highest score so far in the competition, and they devastated their opposing team. That meant that both *Elite* and *Dance, Inc.* had secured spots in the semi-finals.

A little later it was *Seeds'* turn. With Tony finally in their lineup, the team performed beautifully. They had tough competition, but it was amazing to see how *Seeds* rose to the challenge. They were dancing better than ever before. At Regionals, you had to be your best all the time. There was no margin for error.

Emily saw West watching his former team. She wondered what was going on his head. It was normally hard to know what was going on in his weird head anyway. But this must be weird even for West. He had the look of a proud parent. And it was completely warranted, because *Seeds* easily won their round.

Now the three teams moving on to semi-finals had been decided. All that was left was the wildcard spot.

"How did this work again?" Chloe asked West.

"They take the overall top three scoring teams, and the judges decide which team deserves the wildcard spot." West whispered back.

"Oh, well then, we've got this." James told everyone.

But Emily was not so sure. Both of the other teams that were eligible for a wildcard spot performed amazingly as well. Emily just had to hope that the judges thought *The Next Step* was the best team to get the wildcard spot.

"The other teams were good. I'll give them that."

James said. "But they don't have what we have. They don't have the team, they don't have the drive, and they're nowhere near as cool as we are." James laughed.

Before anyone could say anything, the three top-scoring teams were asked to take the stage and line up. Every team member on stage, including *The Next Step*, was nervous. Emily looked around her. She had come so far and gone through so much. Was it all to end now?

"The team that will be facing *Seeds* in the semi-final round is…" Emily put her arm around Michelle and smiled at her. She was glad that they had done this together, as Co-Captains. Whatever happened, at least she had Michelle as a friend. That was worth the world.

"*The Next Step*!" the announcer called out.

Emily felt her heart swell! They had done it! Despite

all of their setbacks and problems along the way, they had come together as a team, and made it all the way to the semi-final round of Regionals.

The Next Step dancers came off the stage to a round of applause from the Seeds dancers. Emily appreciated their congratulations. Without The Next Step, Seeds would never have made it to semi-finals. And without Seeds, The Next Step would never have had West.

Emily was just glad she didn't have to go against Elite. At least, not yet.

# CHAPTER 17
## Eldon

Eldon smiled at Michelle as she counted the dancers through the routine. They only had to win one more round, and they would make it into the finals. And it would be against *Elite*.

*Elite* had gone against *Dance, Inc.* in their semi-final round. And *Elite* had easily beat them. Even though *Dance Inc.* was so good, it was hardly even a fair match.

And now, *Elite* was doing everything they could to scare *The Next Step*, including walking directly through *The Next Step's* practice area. As if it wasn't perfectly obvious that ten people were dancing there.

"Be careful!" Michelle called out.

"Aw… cute costumes, guys! Is your grandma missing her curtains?" Amanda said, smiling evilly at *The Next Step* dancers. And then Amanda looked right at Emily. "And who did your make-up, a clown?"

Eldon knew that would sting Emily. She had spent weeks trying to decide on the perfect Regionals' costume, and even though they had all agreed they were perfect, Emily would still feel like she had failed.

"Honestly, you guys should quit now and join the circus. I think you'd fit in much better there." Amanda said, laughing in Emily's face. "I'm glad you finally found a team you can keep up with, Emily."

"Amanda?" Michelle said, coming to Emily's rescue, "Don't you have your own team to torment?"

"What, Emily can't stick up for herself?" Amanda said,

turning on Michelle.

"You can go now." Michelle said, stepping up to face Amanda.

"Whatever." Amanda said, rolling her eyes and following after her teammates.

Eldon was really impressed with how Michelle had handled Amanda. She hadn't gotten scared, or even mean. She had just been assertive and in charge, like a good Dance Captain should be.

"Eldon? Aren't you going to go talk to her?" Riley asked. Eldon wasn't sure what she was talking about.

But then Eldon noticed that Emily wasn't standing with them anymore. He looked around and saw her seated on a bench. It looked like she was crying.

"Well, I don't know what to do!" Eldon told Riley.

"She's your girlfriend, so go talk to her." Riley replied.

Eldon looked at the other dancers. They all seemed to expect him to go check on Emily. He wished he could tell them that he had actually forgotten he was Emily's boyfriend. He was too busy imagining what his first date with Michelle might be like.

But Michelle wouldn't even meet his eyes. She was staring at the ground, like she was counting how many threads were in the carpet.

"Come on, Eldon, go." Chloe said, giving him a push in Emily's direction.

Eldon waited until his back was turned to them, before rolling his eyes. He so didn't want to do this. He walked over to the bench where Emily was sitting.

As Eldon sat down beside Emily, he felt like the worst boyfriend in the world. He had spent years trying to get Emily to date him, but now he felt like there was nothing that connected him to her at all. Everything felt different now. He felt different now.

"Just ignore Amanda." Eldon told Emily. "She's just mad you came back to *The Next Step*."

"Eldon, there's more to it than that." Emily said sadly.

Eldon took a deep breath. Did Emily know how he felt about Michelle?

"Watching the way Amanda acts, watching the way she talks to people, it just reminds me of the old me." Emily said sadly. "I'm worried that if I get in a confrontation with her, the old Emily will come screaming back out. And I don't want that."

"I know you're strong enough to get through this." Eldon said, sliding towards Emily. Eldon knew he should be doing more to comfort her, but he didn't want to give Emily the wrong impression. Eldon put his arm around Emily, and patted her on the shoulder politely.

"Do you really believe in me?" Emily asked him.

"Yeah." Eldon answered. He did believe in her, the way any good friend would.

As Emily stared at him, he hoped she wouldn't ask any more of him. But Emily moved towards him, and suddenly Eldon realized if he didn't say something quickly, she would kiss him. And Eldon didn't know if he had the heart to kiss her back. So when Emily went to kiss him, Eldon dodged her lips, and brought Emily into a hug. He could not kiss Emily. Not anymore.

# CHAPTER 18

# James

James stood on the side of the stage next to West, watching *Seeds* perform. After they had let West perform with *Seeds*, their tenth dancer had shown up in time to move them into the third round, and then the semi-finals.

And now *The Next Step* had to go against them.

The problem was, *Seeds* was amazing. They were hitting every move and blowing everyone away with their tricks. They had gone from a simple street crew, to a team that had a real chance at winning Regionals.

"Hey, man, is it going to be weird to dance against your old team?" James asked West.

"No," West answered, "I'm pretty weird already, so this situation barely even registers on West's Weird Scale."

James laughed. He wasn't sure if West was serious or joking, but he didn't care. That's what he loved about his friend.

"In the semi-final round, *Seeds* scores ninety-one points!" the announcer called out.

James shared a worried look with West. Ninety-one points was higher than *The Next Step* had ever scored in the entire competition.

As the *Seeds* dancers came off the stage, Emily called the dancers into a huddle. Emily nodded at Michelle.

"Look, guys, it's really important that you dance with passion!" Michelle told them, starting a pep talk.

"That's passion with three 'S's." James joked, trying to

lighten the mood.

"We've already come so far, not only as separate people, but also as--"

"A team!" James said, jumping in and cutting off Emily.

"Take this seriously, James!" Riley yelled at him. Why did she have to get so uptight? He was only trying to make everyone loosen up a little bit.

James was starting to feel like Riley didn't understand him at all. The entire time they had been at Regionals, she had been on his case, constantly telling him to take things seriously.

He was taking things seriously. He was dancing better than he had ever danced before. But he wasn't going to let the pressures of the competition get to him. That just wasn't who he was.

James put Riley out of his mind as he walked onto the stage. They had to kill this round if they wanted to beat *Seeds* and make it into the finals.

They all took their opening positions, the music started, and they started to dance. And after several counts of eight, James realized they had never performed this well. Every member of A-Troupe was giving it all they had. This was their last performance for the day. All they had to do

was push through this last routine, and give it everything they had, and James knew they would make it to finals.

As they struck their final pose, James knew they couldn't have done their routine any better. The entire auditorium burst into applause, and some people even got on their feet. They were getting a standing ovation.

Kate was waiting for them at the side of the stage. They all crowded around her into a giant group hug. If this was their last moment at Regionals, at least it was perfect.

"Almost perfect." James thought, as he felt Riley's hand tug him away from the celebrations. "Come on! Don't you want to celebrate?" James asked her, trying to pull her back to the others.

"Just wait." Riley said, pulling him back to her. This time he didn't fight her. "I just wanted to say I'm sorry for today." Riley told him, looking him straight in the eyes.

"Don't even worry about it." James told her with a smile. But he appreciated her apology. It made James realize that it wasn't that she didn't understand him, it was that she didn't take his jokes very well when she was under stress.

"But if I were to send you a text message, it would say, 'This is who I am. LOL. Winkey face.'" James said.

"What?" Riley said, a confused look on her face.

"I don't stress over things. You've got to accept that." James said, telling Riley the truth.

"Okay. I can live with that." Riley said, smiling up at him. "But you also have to know who you're dating. Because I do stress." Riley answered.

"Can you send me that in a text message?" James joked, picking Riley up and spinning her around.

Before Riley could even laugh, the announcer spoke. "Will *The Next Step* take the stage to receive their score."

James put Riley down and, hand-in-hand, they made their way to the stage with the rest of their team. They were about to find out whether or not they were going to finals.

"In their semi-final round, *The Next Step* scores… ninety-three points, winning the round and moving them into the final competition."

But James had not heard anything past ninety-three points. He was too busy celebrating with his team. They had done it. *The Next Step* was going to finals. They were finally going to dance against *Elite*.

# CHAPTER 19

## Emily

"You guys did a phenomenal job with the first routine yesterday. It was amazing!" Kate congratulated the dancers.

After a good night's sleep, A-Troupe was back on the Regionals' stage, bright and early, ready to rehearse their final routine.

"But this is finals, so we need to up our game in this second routine." Kate said, getting serious.

It was a hard choice, deciding on which routine they were going to use first. Teams like *Elite* saved their best routine for last, hoping that when they got to finals, they would have a better routine in their back pocket.

But *The Next Step* had gone the other way, deciding to use their best routine first. It's how they got themselves to finals. Now they had to find a way to make their not-so-good routine, their better routine. And they only had a few hours. Emily knew their second routine wasn't up to snuff.

"I have something to tell you guys." Emily said to the other dancers. She knew some things about *Elite's* second routine that she had kept to herself. She didn't want to freak out the other dancers any more than they already were. But now that they were going against *Elite*, it was time Emily told them the truth.

"*Elite* has an airplane in their final performance." Emily said quickly, like she was trying to rip off a bandage as painlessly as possible.

"Of course Lucien would have a plane on the stage."

61

Kate said in disbelief.

"How big of a plane?" Giselle asked.

"It's a big plane." Emily said seriously.

"Oooh!" West said, his hand shooting into the air. Emily already knew what his question was going to be.

"West, it's a prop plane." Emily responded.

"You mean with propellers?" West asked.

"No, I mean it's not real." Emily said slowly, hoping he would finally understand.

"Well, I guess that makes sense." West said after thinking about it for a moment. "I was wondering how they would get an entire plane into this building."

Emily laughed along with the rest of her team. West certainly knew how to make the tension disappear.

"We can't worry about what anyone else is doing." James said to the team. "We can only worry about ourselves."

"But how are we going to top an airplane?" Michelle asked.

"A prop airplane." West said, making them all laugh again.

"All planes aside, I think we should focus on Michelle and Eldon's duet." Chloe offered.

Emily felt her stomach knot. There was something about Michelle and Eldon working together that she didn't like.

"Actually, that's a genius idea. We could move the duet from the middle of the dance to the beginning. It will be so much more powerful there." Kate said, speaking a mile-a-minute. It seemed liked everyone was inspired by the duet idea.

"I'm just not sure if a duet will really be enough to counter a plane." Emily said, hoping everyone would understand.

"Uh, yeah it will! Have you seen it?" James asked her.

"Their duet is amazing." Riley added.

"It's so emotional." Chloe said, in support of her own idea.

"Is this what everyone wants?" Emily asked.

"Yeah!" Her entire team responded.

If they all wanted to feature the duet, there was nothing Emily could do about it. 'New Emily' was a team player. But that didn't mean she wouldn't keep an eye on Michelle and Eldon. She had been noticing something between them, and the last thing Emily wanted to do was watch her boyfriend dance a lovers' duet with someone else.

"Consider it done." Emily said, "But this is Regionals, and that duet requires a lot of chemistry. Do you think you guys can fake it?" Emily asked, crossing her arms.

She watched as Eldon and Michelle shared a look. She could see it in both of their eyes. They weren't faking anything.

"I think so." Eldon said, breaking eye contact with Michelle.

"Yeah." Michelle said, blushing slightly and looking

down.

They had chemistry, all right. "All right then." Emily said, giving up. She wasn't oblivious. She knew what was going on. And the last thing she wanted was for Eldon and Michelle to get up on stage, in front of an audience, and display whatever was going on between them.

# CHAPTER 20

# Eldon

Eldon could not believe his luck. Having his duet with Michelle, and it being the focus of their final dance, meant he could spend extra time with Michelle, without making Emily suspicious. Eldon did not want to hurt Emily. He still cared about her and probably always would. Emily was his first love. But Michelle was his second. Maybe his true love.

As he danced with Michelle, he only became more sure of his decision. It was the right one. She was an amazing partner, both in dance and in life. Now all he had to do was tell her.

"That was good." Michelle said, as Eldon spun her towards him and into his arms.

"By the way," Eldon said, unable to keep it to himself anymore, "you are all I think about. I want to be with you."

Michelle looked at him for a moment without speaking.

"Really?" Michelle asked, a small smile spreading across her face.

"Yeah." Eldon said, smiling back. "If we really want to be together, then we should be allowed to be together."

"But what about…?" Michelle asked, trailing off as she looked over at Emily.

"I don't think Emily should come between us anymore. If I like you more than I like her, then I think I need to be with you." Eldon said.

Michelle was smiling widely now. He knew she felt

the same way he did, but they had to be careful. If anyone found out now, it could ruin everything for *The Next Step*.

"I just hope it doesn't mess anything up for the team." Michelle said, worried.

"I think I should wait to tell her until after Regionals." Eldon said, being honest with Michelle.

"Good idea. Let's just focus on the competition, and we can talk about it later." Michelle agreed.

"Okay. But just so you know, I can't wait to take you on our first date." Eldon said, grabbing Michelle's hand, spinning her around, and dipping her.

As Eldon pulled Michelle back up to standing position, they both began laughing. He hadn't had this much fun dancing with anyone else.

"Michelle?" Eldon heard Emily say behind him. "Could I talk to Eldon for a second?"

Michelle gave Eldon a quick look, and then headed off without a word. There was nothing they could say to Emily. Not right now anyway.

"I was just wondering if we could talk for a few minutes?" Emily asked him quietly. But he did not have anything to say to her.

"I'm kind of having trouble with the choreography."

Eldon lied.

"You never have trouble with choreography." Emily reminded him.

"Yeah, but this is all new choreography, and I just want to make sure I get it right.  You know, for finals."  Eldon said, hiding his feelings.  "Is that okay?" he asked Emily, trying to sound like the caring boyfriend he used to be.

"Yeah," Emily said, looking down, "that's fine.  We can talk later."

"Thanks." Eldon said, turning away from her to find Michelle.

He knew she deserved better treatment than the way he was acting, but he could not be honest with her, and he could not lie to her.  So the best thing for him to do was ignore her altogether.

# CHAPTER 21

# James

J ames and the other dancers stood in the wings as the *Elite* dancers rushed around preparing for their final routine. It was true. *Elite* did have a plane in their routine. A giant plane backdrop that filled up the entire back-half of the stage. As well, there was a rotating platform with seats, to imitate the inside of a cockpit.

All of the *Elite* girls were decked out in glittery flight attendant uniforms, while the boys were dressed like pilots. There was clearly a theme emerging.

But the glitter and glamour was nothing compared to the routine. It was the perfect competition routine, full of clean lines and group choreography. "Woah." he heard Riley say quietly, as one of the *Elite* boys flipped off of another one's shoulders, landing perfectly into *Elite*'s final pose.

Watching *Elite* get a standing ovation made James feel like the bar was set so high, he couldn't see it anymore. As the *Elite* dancers headed off stage, he looked around at the other A-Troupe dancers, and he could see how nervous they all were.

"Okay, guys, bring it in." he called out to his team. James knew that if they felt as nervous as he did, he might be able to rally them a little bit.

"On the count of three… One, two, three!" James called out, putting his hand into the middle of the circle with everyone else's.

"*The Next Step*!" they all cheered.

The curtain dropped, and *The Next Step* dancers headed out on stage to start warming up. But James stayed back with Riley.

They stood beside each other, silently. James looked down at Riley. Out of all the people in the world, James was glad he got to be here with her.

"May I have this dance?" Riley asked. She turned around to face him, offering him her hand. But then, just as quickly, she withdrew it. "What is she doing here?" Riley asked, the colour draining from her face.

James turned around to see Beth standing in the wings, waving at him. What *was* she doing here? They had been broken up for over a year, but Beth still didn't seem to get the hint that James had moved on.

"Just give me one second." he said to Riley, who by now had her arms crossed. "Don't worry about it. I'll be right back."

Riley didn't look happy. And James didn't blame her. They had just agreed to accept each other as they were, but James knew Beth wasn't part of that deal.

"What are you doing here?" James asked Beth, whispering to encourage her to talk quietly. Because talking quietly was not something Beth was good at doing.

"Aren't you excited to see me?" she asked, looking up at him with her typical Beth smile.

"Yeah, sure, but I have to focus on the dance. We're about to perform." James said, trying to be kind.

"I'm so excited to be here!" Beth said, reaching out to touch his arm.

James shrugged her off, and smiled, not wanting to hurt her feelings.

"When I found out you made it to finals, I knew I had to come support you!" Beth told him.

"How did you get here?" James asked her. He appreciated her support, but he wished Beth would get he was with Riley now.

"I took a bus." Beth said with a smile. "Okay, I took two buses. It was like, eight hours, but it was all worth it, to see you here!"

James looked back to where Riley was pretending to warm up, but James knew she was trying to listen in on their conversation. "Okay, well, thanks for coming up. I gotta get out there." James said, trying to remove himself from the situation as gracefully as possible.

"Wait!" Beth said, grabbing his shoulder to stop him. "I've been thinking about it the whole way here, and I just have to tell you, so you know."

Beth stopped talking and looked down at the floor. James didn't know what was coming next, but he was pretty sure he didn't want to know.

"I still love you." Beth said, looking him in the eyes, determined. "You don't have to say anything back. I just needed you to know."

James didn't know what to say. He would always care about her: Beth was the first girl he ever said he loved. But that was before he understood what love really was. It was before he knew Riley.

"I really have to get back on stage." James said, backing away from Beth.

"Just think about it, okay?" she called after him. "Good luck! I'll be watching you!"

James turned around and headed onto the stage.

"So? What did she say?" Riley asked him.

"Nothing. She just wanted to tell me she was here to watch." James told her.

"That's it?" Riley asked, tilting her head to the side.

"Yeah." James lied. "That's it."

He didn't need to tell Riley the whole truth. He knew that a poorly-timed truth did more harm than it did good. Telling Riley what Beth had said, right before they went on stage, would take Riley's head out of the competition completely. James had no doubt about that. And right now, they needed to stay focused. This was their only chance to make it to Nationals.

# CHAPTER 22

## Emily

Emily paced back and forth on the stage, running through the routine in her head. As she looked around the stage at the rest of her team, she realized how excited she was to perform.

As Michelle caught her eye and gave her a thumbs-up, Emily smiled. They had finally made it, all the way to the Regional finals. If they could completely ace this routine, and blow the judges away, they had a real shot at beating *Elite*.

That would mean they would be on their way to the Nationals, Emily thought, as she turned around to pace the other way.

Every year, the winner of each region got to participate in the *Absolute Dance Nationals*. And the winner of that competition went on to Internationals, where they got to compete against the best dance studios in the world.

But Emily was getting ahead of herself. She just had to focus on Regionals right now. And if they were lucky and won, then Emily could let her head spin about Nationals, and Internationals, and Galactics, or whatever came after Internationals.

Emily turned around towards Michelle to tell her the joke about the *Galactic Dance Championships* when she saw it. Michelle and Eldon were hugging. It wasn't a friendly, quick, good luck hug. It was a long, lingering, more-than-a-friend hug. Emily had to look away.

This wasn't the first time she had seen Michelle and

Eldon getting close. She had first noticed something between them when she came back to *The Next Step* from *Elite*, but she had always pushed it to the back of her mind. She didn't want it to be true.

But now she felt like they weren't even being secretive about their feelings anymore. If Emily had noticed, surely other members of A-Troupe had, too. Emily had to find out the truth, once and for all. She had to ask Eldon what was going on.

"Eldon," Emily asked, as he silently walked by her, "Can I talk to you for a minute?"

"I just want to--" Eldon said, trying to avoid conversation.

"Focus on the routine, I know." Emily said, cutting him off. She grabbed his arm and dragged him to the side of the stage. He had already embarrassed her enough. She didn't need him to declare his love for someone else in public.

"I need you to tell me what is going on." Emily said.

"I really don't want to talk about this right now." Eldon said, trying to pull away from her.

"Eldon!" Emily snapped.

"What?" he asked her, as if he didn't know.

Emily took a moment to collect herself. She didn't want to fight with Eldon, she just wanted him to tell her the truth. "Eldon," she said more calmly, taking his hands in hers, "do you have feelings for Michelle?"

"Emily, can we please not talk about this right now?" Eldon asked.

He didn't deny it. Not for one second. Emily already had her answer. But she still wanted to hear him say it.

"Eldon, please," she pleaded with him quietly, "do you have feelings for her?"

Eldon thought for a few seconds. But it was not long enough, because he answered her, and he shouldn't have done that. "Yes. I want to be with Michelle."

Emily was utterly and totally crushed. But she would never, ever give him the satisfaction of seeing how much.

"It's fine." Emily lied, with the bravest smile she could muster. She felt like her heart was a balloon, and Eldon had just stuck a pin in it. The pain slowly poured out of her, and there was no way to stop it. It was unbearable. The only comfort she ever had was in Eldon. And now, he wasn't even hers anymore. He was Michelle's.

"Thirty seconds until curtain!" Kate called out, "Everyone get into their spots!"

Without a second look back at her, Eldon moved to his spot on the stage. But Emily felt like she was frozen: a stone-cold statue, with a broken heart.

"Emily!" Stephanie called out, waking her up from her stupor.

Emily stumbled into her spot beneath the platform. Staring at Eldon, she hoped he would look back at her one last time. She hoped he might still have some tiny feelings for her. But as the music started, and the curtains rose, Eldon was only looking at Michelle.

# CHAPTER 23

## Michelle

Michelle walked down the platform towards Eldon. She was so excited knowing that their first dance together would be as boyfriend and girlfriend. And it would be on the Regionals' stage.

Jumping into Eldon's arms, Michelle had never felt so safe. Not only was he her boyfriend, but he was also the perfect dance partner. She didn't trust anyone in the world as much as she trusted Eldon.

And now that Michelle knew that she and Eldon were finally going to be together, this dance was the perfect start to their relationship.

## Emily

Emily had never thought about the irony of the dance until now. Eldon as Romeo, and Michelle as Juliette, kept apart by the people they love. But eventually, everyone

75

realizes how in love they are, and true love wins out in the end.

Emily had actually read *Romeo and Juliette*, and in the book, there were a lot of casualties. And she was one of them. Emily wished she could be anywhere else than on the Regionals' stage, but she had no choice but to smile big and dance her hardest. That's what a professional dancer did. And that's what her team needed of her. So that's what Emily did. And it might have been the bravest thing she ever did.

# West

West was having the time of his life. He had never danced so hard, or jumped so high. As he prepared himself for a trick, he gave a small nod to James and Eldon. He needed them to be ready. He ran towards Eldon, scurrying up his chest, doing a backflip, and landing on the floor. It was just in time for James to leap over him. The crowd exploded in cheers.

In the short time he had been at *The Next Step*, he had grown so much as a dancer, both technically and in his tricks. It was thanks in large part to James and Eldon. The three boys were always pushing each other to create better and cooler tricks. And James and Eldon were always helping West stay technically accurate. Yup, West was having the time of his life.

# Chloe

Chloe had never been more glad to be anywhere in her life. She couldn't believe that, for a time, she thought she would be okay to miss Regionals. Chloe vowed never to quit dance, ever again. She belonged on that stage. She could tell by how well the audience was reacting to her dancing, to her team's dancing.

She was so grateful to her friends for supporting her through the hard times, and even stepping up to support

her financially.  When it came down to it, Chloe was the luckiest girl alive to have friends like the dancers at *The Next Step*.

# Giselle

Giselle was dancing at half speed with the other dancers.  They danced in slow motion, as Michelle and Eldon moved at full speed above them.  The other dancers moved slowly, representing how slowly they acknowledged the true love of Michelle and Eldon.  By the time the other dancers began dancing at full speed, they had finally come around and were ready to dance in support of Michelle and Eldon.

Giselle was so proud of herself.  As she danced, she thought of Daniel.  She wished her best friend could be on the Regionals' stage with her, but instead he was injured and at home.  Knowing this, how special it was to be where she was, Giselle danced twice as hard as she ever had.  She danced in honour of Daniel.

# Stephanie

Stephanie ran across the stage, fabric held high over her head. It was her idea to add swaths of fabrics to their performance. And it was working.

Stephanie had found that once she was able to see herself as her own person, outside of Emily, she was also able to become more creative. She had a better understanding of her own mind now, and she had so many ideas that she wanted to explore. She might be a singer. She might be an actor. But she was for sure a dancer. And right now, she felt her best, dancing on stage with all of her friends.

# Tiffany

All the drama that had come before Regionals was forgotten as soon as Tiffany stepped on stage. Forgotten was the new girl who had arrived and set off a chain of events that included the end of the E-Girls, Emily and Stephanie leaving the studio, and then coming back, and Michelle and Emily somehow becoming Co-Captains. It was a lot. But at this moment, there was only dance.

# Riley

Riley danced across the stage in the group choreography. She was so proud of how far her team had come. She was so proud of how far she had come. Riley had finally become a person. And she was so proud of that.

But she wasn't sure if she would have been able to do any of it, without James's help. He had been there for her, every step of the way. Sure, he could be frustrating, but he could also be amazing, and supportive, and trustworthy. Riley knew she had nothing to worry about. James was her boyfriend, no one else's. They both made each other stronger.

# James

As James backflipped off the top of the platform, landing on the ground, and making his way to his final position, he knew *The Next Step* had killed it. No one had missed a step, every trick had gone off without a hitch, and the energy radiating off *The Next Step* dancers was powerful.

If they didn't win, then James didn't know good dancing. But that was one thing James did know. James also knew how he felt about Riley. In the middle of the dance, he glanced over at her and smiled. She was so strong, so full of life. It's what had attracted him to Riley in the first place. This quiet girl who didn't know how powerful she was. From the moment James had met Riley, she had been the only girl in whom he had been interested, and he didn't think that would ever change.

# Eldon

Eldon took Michelle's hand, and ran up the ramp to the top of the platform. Now that he had told Emily the truth, he felt like he was finally free to dance with Michelle with his full emotions. He didn't have to hide how he felt about Michelle, and he could show that in his dancing.

As the final few beats of the *Stand Up* played, Eldon dipped Michelle down and then brought her back up to meet his eyes. As much as he wanted to share this moment with his team, he also wanted to have it with Michelle. As the song ended, it was the moment that their relationship officially began.

# CHAPTER 24

## Michelle

Michelle stared into Eldon's eyes. She could hardly look away. All she cared about was Eldon, and the way he was looking at her. But when she heard thunderous applause coming from the audience, and the crowd jump to its feet, she had to look away. Besides, staring at him any longer was making her cheeks flush red.

Eldon held his hand out for Michelle, and she looked down at it. Smiling, she took it, and the two of them walked down the platform towards the rest of the team.

As they joined everyone else, *The Next Step* dancers all took a final bow. Michelle felt amazing. If this was the last time she ever got to stand on a stage, this feeling would be enough for her.

The audience stood on their feet, applauding for *The Next Step*. Michelle felt Eldon squeeze her hand. She looked at him with a smile.

"Just so you know, I told Emily about us being together." Eldon said quietly.

Michelle's stomach dropped. One moment she had been over the moon with their Regionals' performance, and now she was suddenly worried sick.

"I thought we decided to wait until after the competition?" Michelle asked, confused. Why would Eldon do something like that to Emily?

"She knew what was going on. She cornered me before the dance, and forced it out of me. I know we were going to wait. I'm sorry." Eldon said, looking Michelle dead in the eyes.

Michelle understood. She knew how demanding Emily could be. If their places had been reversed, Michelle would have wanted to know what was going on as well.

They couldn't discuss it any more because the *Elite* dancers joined *The Next Step* team on stage, ready to be judged. In this round, no scores were awarded. It was just about who was the best. So all that was left was determining who would be named Regionals' champions.

Michelle squeezed Eldon's hand, and he squeezed back. She was glad that she had him here with her. If they won, then everything Michelle had done for the team was the right choice. But if they lost, all the pain and heartbreak she caused, will have been for nothing.

"Ladies and gentlemen…" the announcer called out. "The winner of the *Absolute Dance Regional Championships*, region fourteen, is…"

Michelle looked down the line of dancers that made up her team. Every single one of them deserved to be standing on that stage. Every single one of them deserved to win.

"*The Next Step*!" the announcer called out.

They had won!

*The Next Step* were Regionals' champions!

Michelle screamed, and she and Eldon shared a hug. She couldn't believe it. Everything she had done had been the right decision. Everything she had done had led them to this moment, this winning moment.

Michelle let go of Eldon, and joined the other dancers in a giant group hug. Kate even ran out from the wings and joined them. They weren't going to stand on ceremony anymore. They were *The Next Step*. They were Regionals' champions. And this was their stage.

As the judges came out on stage with the trophy, Michelle found Emily. The two girls hoisted the trophy, high into the air. Michelle smiled at Emily, but Emily didn't return the smile.

"Are we okay?" Michelle asked, as the girls lowered the trophy. Michelle knew she had to talk to Emily now, before things got any worse.

But Emily didn't respond. She just pulled the trophy out of Michelle's hands and headed off to celebrate with the others.

The excitement drained from Michelle's body. This is exactly what she didn't want to have happen. Now that Emily had found out that Eldon wanted to be with Michelle, there was no telling what she would do next.

"*The Next Step!  The Next Step!*"  The crowd cheered, as Michelle tried to join in.  But she couldn't get excited anymore, because, as she gave Emily another glance, Emily gave her back the most evil look possible.

From that moment, Michelle knew that things at *The Next Step* would never be the same.

## COMING SOON

# THE NEXT STEP

## Road to Nationals